Wonderful Willow

Discovering Your Identity as a Precious Child of God

Tammy Schwartz

Published in the United States of America by Be Still
Christian Publishing House

First Edition

ISBN: 978-0-9993996-0-6

*To my cousin Lisa—
God is your refuge and strength.
You are His masterpiece.*

Contents

INTRODUCTION

"You saw me before I was born.
Every day of my life was recorded in your book.
Every moment was laid out before a single day had
passed." (Psalm 139:16 NLT)

There once was (always has been and always will be) an all-knowing and all-powerful Creator. He carefully and masterfully designed each one of His children in His own image. He loved every son and daughter He made. He formed them with His hands, breathed life into them, and promised to walk with them on their life journeys. He gave them a Book of Instructions filled with His words. The Creator's Spirit enabled His precious children to understand and believe the words inside. His Book of Instructions taught them how they should live. It also told them about the Creator's Son and how He made a way for them to receive their Great Eternal Reward.

The Creator's children were given a beautiful place to live filled with stunning mountains, gentle streams, soft furry animals, and starry skies. He fashioned them to see, hear, taste, touch, and smell. He provided colors, music, temperature, textures, and time. They could laugh, cry, love, dream, dance, and sing. He also gave them the ability to communicate with each other and with Him. He loved nothing more than to hear the sound of their voices praising and calling out to Him.

Each child held a special purpose only they could fulfill. They were given the interests, experiences, and abilities needed to accomplish the purpose set before them. The Creator's children were brilliantly designed and beautifully complex.

Unfortunately, not every child of the Creator believed they were a masterpiece. Many could not see beyond their own flaws and mistakes. They felt unimportant and broken. This is the story of one such child, Willow, and how the Creator helped her to discover her true beauty and value.

May God use this story to help you understand that you also are His child—loved and treasured. You hold His purpose that is yours alone.

1

WILLOW'S NEW PATH

The birds sang, delicate wildflowers swayed in the breeze, and an occasional puffy white cloud drifted across the bright blue sky. The days seemed flawless. Willow felt safe as she walked down the level path with her Creator at her side. He provided strength and a sense of security. She knew He would help her face whatever challenges lay ahead. As she stopped to rest for a moment, she could not help but recall the remarkable way the Creator led her to the beautiful place where she stood…

You see, Willow's journey had not always been easy. She had experienced numerous joys but she had also faced difficult challenges. Rather than turning to the Creator for help, she spent years struggling to get by on her own. She became burdened and exhausted. The day she encountered a great big rock blocking her path was a day that changed her life forever.

Willow struggled to move the rock on her own. The Creator watched patiently. He longed for her to reach out to Him but she did not. Despite all of her calculated attempts, the rock would not budge.

Feeling defeated, Willow finally recognized her need for help and called to the Creator. He patiently offered the guidance she desperately needed. One by one, He gave her courage to release every detail (joys and burdens) over to Him.

The Creator also opened Willow's eyes to see her need for Jesus. He was not only her Savior and Friend, but He was her Strong Rock—the One she could lean on for strength.

Not long after Willow surrendered to the Lord, she was lifted easily up and over the great big rock. The Creator set her on a new path—the place where she was now standing.

Willow looked around at her beautiful surroundings. She felt relief when she noticed the path ahead was smooth and straight. She felt even more reassurance in knowing she would not walk alone. The Creator loved her and would never leave her. He enjoyed their time together even more than she did. He smiled every time He looked into her heart and felt the trust she had in Him.

2

A NEW PURPOSE

"Praise be to the God and Father of our Lord Jesus
Christ, the Father of compassion and the God of all
comfort, who comforts us in all our troubles, so that we
can comfort those in any trouble with the comfort we
ourselves receive from God. For just as we share
abundantly in the sufferings of Christ, so also our
comfort abounds through Christ."
(1 Corinthians 1:3–5 NIV)

The Creator arranged many opportunities for Willow to
share the lessons she had learned. She considered it a
privilege to help. The Creator delighted in hearing her say,
"Thank you for allowing me to experience the joy of
comforting others with the same comfort I have received
from you."

Willow was soon instructed to do more than simply speak
to those in need. The Creator's Spirit encouraged her to
write down the treasured lessons she had learned. She
always enjoyed writing. (The Creator knew this better
than anyone since He was, after all, her Maker and the
Giver of all good gifts). Willow was excited to begin. The
words flowed quickly and easily. In a relatively short
amount of time, her story was finished. She wrote about
the heavy bag of details she carried, the damaging effects
of the dark snake's lies, and the beautiful truths spoken by
the Creator. She felt privileged to share her account and
yet, at the same time, she was concerned about how her
friends would react to some of her longtime secrets.

Despite her concerns, she followed the Spirit's direction and began to tell her story.

Willow found it remarkable that her friends were not angry, nor did they judge. Rather, they were encouraged and inspired, especially by the Creator's kind words. Some were moved to tears. Willow's story carried a message urgently needed by many of the Creator's dear children and some of her closest friends.

3

AN OLD ENEMY

Truth be told, Willow was amazed by the reactions to her story. The compliments felt good. As she allowed a small amount of pride to enter her heart, a shadow of darkness stole her focus. She unintentionally took her eyes off of the Creator just long enough to get a glimpse of an old enemy. The deceitful dark snake that slithered by had caused so much pain in her past. She noticed on his back a tiny piece of glass that looked familiar. She recognized it as a remaining shard from the broken Mirror of Comparison.

Years earlier, the dark snake had slipped an evil mirror into Willow's heavy bag of details. When she looked into it, she could easily identify her flaws. It also helped her compare herself to others. She always came out on the losing end. The Creator had helped Willow to shatter this mirror following her struggle against the great big rock.

Though the mirror fragment was small, its effect on Willow was, unfortunately, enormous. It shifted her attention away from the Creator and her newfound purpose. She began to think about her faults and all the years she was not truthful with her friends. She no longer felt worthy of their forgiveness. "What about the years of hiding? Why would they forgive me?" She asked. The snake smirked over his easy success. Willow felt shame over past mistakes and sorrow for momentarily taking her eyes off of the Creator.

Her path descended down a small hill. That may not sound worthy of mentioning, but it was the first change

Willow had experienced in her level path since she had been lifted up and over the great big rock. Willow became concerned about the change in elevation.

As she walked the downward slope, she began to feel tired and weary. Thankfully, she quickly recognized her need for help and paused for a moment to pray. The Creator rejoiced. The dark snake slid under the nearest bush to hide from the Light.

The Creator led Willow out of the hollow and up to a small bench resting on a nearby hill. The sun shone over vast fields filled with tiny bright yellow flowers. Her anxiety melted away.

"Willow, you chose wisely when you called to Me for help," He said. "Always remember that I am here for you."

She thanked Him and said, "I am disappointed in myself. I make the same mistakes over and over. I felt secure walking side by side with You. I was really glad that we had been so close."

He interrupted her "My dear child, we still are close."

She carried on. "I know—I guess I just don't feel I deserve Your forgiveness. I had been keeping my eyes fixed on You and You were leading the way down the path. Then—with only the slightest distraction—I took my eyes off of You. Why would I do that? I have seen Your goodness. I have felt Your love. It doesn't make sense. I gave into temptation—again! How can You continue to love me?"

The Creator gently answered, "Willow, My love for you does not waiver based on your actions or mistakes. You are My child. I formed you in your mother's womb. I have great plans for you. You have been forgiven and restored. The punishment for your sin was laid upon My Son, Jesus. My Spirit lives within you and guides you as you desire to change. Rest in My ability, not in your own. You are loved, now and always. Nothing you do or don't do will ever change that. It is that simple."

"But I don't think I deserve to be forgiven," Willow continued.

In an effort to help her see the truth, the Creator asked her a question. "Would you tell me about one of the most meaningful gifts you ever received?"

Willow thought about it and answered, "My aunt made a quilt for me years ago. She carefully chose colors that would match my furniture. She spent many hours working on it. It was an amazing gift."

"I remember the day you received it," He said. "It *was* a gift made with love." Willow agreed.

The Creator asked her to think about the day she was given the quilt and then inquired, "Would you have ever considered rejecting the gift?"

Without hesitation, Willow answered, "Absolutely not! My aunt had me in mind as she put time and effort into creating such an heirloom. Every time I look at it, I am reminded that she loves me. How could I ever turn away a gift like that? Not only would she have been hurt, but I would have missed out on the joy of receiving her beautiful offering."

"You are right," He said and then went on to explain, "Just as you would not want to miss out on the joy of receiving your aunt's gift to you, I do not want you to miss the joy of receiving *My* great gift for you.

My Son, Jesus, lovingly had you in mind as He died on the cross. He suffered and sacrificed His life so that you would be free. He made the way for you to receive the Great Eternal Reward. There is no greater gift. Please do not reject it.

The dark snake lies as he tries to convince you that you are not worthy of being forgiven. He uses guilt and shame to distract you from the peace and freedom you are meant to enjoy.

The truth is that you are now clean as it says in Isaiah 1:18, 'Though your sins are like scarlet, they shall be as white as snow; though they are red as crimson, they shall be like wool.' (NIV) You are forgiven and free to live the amazing life I have planned for you."

With a grateful heart, Willow accepted the Creator's gift of forgiveness and found that her guilt quickly diminished. She went on to think about her friends and gladly accepted their pardon as well. Her newfound peace gave her an even stronger desire to share the good news of her Creator's love with as many people as possible.

4

A DEEP DARK VALLEY

Willow felt uplifted as she continued to share her story. People would say things like, "I want my daughter to read this," or, "I carry a mirror just like yours," or, "My sister needs to hear this message." She was even asked by one friend, "How is it possible that you wrote a story about *my* life?"

Willow knew that all the glory and credit belonged to her Creator alone. It was His Spirit guiding her every word.

As you would expect, Willow did not only hear compliments. She also heard a few negative comments. One older gentleman went to the effort of mailing a note to tell her that he did not like her story. He was highly critical. Despite all of the positive comments, her mind would not let go of the negative. Her heart was broken by this criticism.

In a weak moment, Willow allowed herself to become offended. At that same moment, she caught movement out of the corner of her eye. Without thinking (or praying), she made the mistake of turning her back on the Creator. This time, she saw a slightly larger piece of mirror lodged between the scales of the dark snake. She read the words written in the glass, "You are not a writer." The wounding words soaked into her being and were accepted as truth. She felt deflated. Her legs fatigued as she began walking down a steep slope.

Distressed by how quickly her strength had been swept away, she ended up low in a valley. Dark trees. Deep mud. Her mood matched her surroundings. She questioned everything about herself, not just her writing. Rather than calling to her Creator for help, she resorted to her comfortable old habits. She decided to rescue herself out of this dark valley.

The best way to lift her mood, she believed, was to seek out more encouragement. So Willow began to share her story with as many people as possible. *She* was leading the way this time with her eyes focused on building herself back up again.

Her plan did help—a little. Most people liked the story and that offered temporary encouragement. But then a strange thing happened. As Willow read to one person after another, she found it more and more difficult to make it to the end of the story because her mouth would become severely dry. She soon found it necessary to carry water with her, not just while reading, but wherever she went. Despite seeing several doctors and trying a number of home remedies, there was no relief to be found.

At this point, Willow faced more than doubts about her ability to write. She now faced an unidentified illness. After losing her voice, teaching and leading meetings at work became almost impossible. She could not even swallow food without drinking water. She knew something was terribly wrong.

As He always did, the Creator steadfastly stood by Willow's side waiting for her to call for help. She was not yet willing.

Willow instead attempted to settle back into one of her busiest seasons at work. She hoped the rush would distract her from the illness, but each week new symptoms developed. Just as she had tried to hide many struggles earlier in her journey, Willow also tried to hide this illness. Finally, when she was barely able to walk, her family, friends, and co-workers became aware of the seriousness of her situation.

Willow did not give in. She struggled every step of the way just as she had after her dad died. The dark snake frequently crossed her now thick, muddy path. She trudged and weaved her way through this lowest of valleys. The snake leered as she battled feelings of despair and hopelessness. Willow was unable to find her way out and, sadly, she felt too submerged to ask for help.

5

PLACE OF REFUGE

Four months into her illness, Willow became too weak to walk the path any longer. She found herself in a great deal of pain, inside and out. She cried deeply, and yet, strangely, no tears fell from her eyes. She then grieved over her loss of tears—another symptom of the illness.

She spoke aloud to herself with a raspy voice, "I can't walk. I can't talk. How can I keep working? I can't write. (She believed the snake's lie.) What good am I anymore? What is my purpose? Why am I still here?"

Willow thought about the special job she had been given by her Creator. She loved teaching children from His Book of Instructions. She felt it a great honor to share the truth regarding the Great Eternal Reward. She especially loved sharing the story about her battle against the great big rock. She recalled the lessons she had learned—Jesus, our Rock, came to save us and is able to help us through any struggle. When we are weak, He remains steady and strong.[1]

Sitting on the muddy ground exhausted and afraid, Willow again wondered how she could have so quickly ended up in such a dark and low place.

Without even realizing it, Willow's questions transitioned very naturally into prayers to her Creator. "I don't understand what is happening to me. I need help, but I

[1] 2 Corinthians 12:9-11

do not want to be a burden. I am sorry for turning away from You. How am I going to make it through? I cannot do this alone."

Willow grasped for her Book of Instructions. With all of her strength, she prayed these words from Psalm 121:

"I lift up my eyes to the mountains—where does my help come from? My help comes from the LORD, the Maker of heaven and earth.

He will not let your foot slip—he who watches over you will not slumber; indeed, he who watches over Israel will neither slumber nor sleep.

The LORD watches over you—the LORD is your shade at your right hand; the sun will not harm you by day, nor the moon by night.

The LORD will keep you from all harm—he will watch over your life; the LORD will watch over your coming and going both now and forevermore." (NIV)

"Creator, please help!" Willow pleaded as she fully outstretched her arms to the heavens as a little girl reaches for her daddy.

Without one full second passing, the Creator made His presence clearly known to her. He heard her cries for help and forgiveness. She had finally spoken the words He longed to hear for many weeks. He celebrated knowing that this hurting and loved child of His would now receive the assistance she urgently needed.

Despite the pain and fatigue, Willow felt a deep sense of relief in knowing that she was no longer alone in this battle. She never was. And so, with the Creator at her side, Willow began a new chapter of healing on her journey.

6

I WILL CARRY YOU

The Creator was well aware of Willow's physical and emotional afflictions. He understood her inability to walk up the steep path and so He gently lifted her. His strength was, for her, a familiar source of comfort and hope.

Compassionately, He carried her up and out of the dark valley. He returned her to the solid path where the two had closely walked together not long ago. The path was a refreshing sight for her weary eyes.

Just as she took in a deep breath of crisp, fresh air, the Creator stepped off the solid path and headed toward a grove of majestic sequoia trees. With each step He took, a new path was being revealed. Willow did not know where their journey would end, but she felt secure in knowing that she was held in the almighty arms of her Creator.

The closer they came to the grove, the larger the trees appeared. Once in the forest, Willow noted that it was not at all dark or frightening. Rays of sunlight shone brightly though the canopy. Even more than that, the Creator's light revealed every colorful detail in this beautifully serene setting. Willow appreciated, more than ever before, the song of the orioles and the faint sound of water trickling down a nearby stream.

The Creator, at last, stopped and spoke to her, "Willow, you need time away to rest. Your body and your spirit are in need of healing. This place of refuge is My gift to you. There are valuable lessons I will teach you during your time here. Trust in Me and learn from Me. When the time is right, we will return to the solid path and continue on your journey together."

The Creator then revealed two homes to Willow on the outer edge of the grove. He allowed her to choose where she would like to stay and rest. The first home was quite large. It would have been impressive by most people's standards. It was located alongside a long and winding stream. Willow noticed a drawback to the first home right away. It was built on a sandy foundation.

The second home was older and simpler. It was a little brick house. You might have used the words "cozy" or "basic" to describe it. The curtains on the windows were opened, revealing a stone fireplace with a crackling fire burning inside. More than anything else, it pleased Willow to see that the second home was built on a foundation of solid rock. Willow knew from experience that the Rock was always the better choice and so she chose to stay in the little brick house.

7

THE RESTING ROOM

The Creator was pleased with Willow's decision. He led her into the first room of the little brick house. The Resting Room, as it would become known, felt soothing and comfortable. It was not large, but contained every item Willow might possibly need.

The gray stone fireplace with the flickering fire had a decorative hand-carved oak mantle. It was similar to one Willow's dad had made in their own home. The polished maple floor glistened except where covered by a thick hazelnut-colored rug. Willow's painful feet felt relief stepping onto the ultra-plush carpet. The walls were painted lilac gray and minimally decorated with one quilt and one mirror. The windows in the front of the house were large and brought in healthy amounts of sunlight. There were no clocks in the entire home. Willow was now moving to her Creator's time, not her own.

A large sturdy bookshelf had been placed to the right of the fireplace. It was filled with a wide variety of books, hand-selected by the Creator. He knew what Willow needed and would enjoy. A bird's eye maple coffee table sat in the middle of the room. As the daughter of a master craftsman, Willow could tell this table was well constructed. It rested just in front of a long and deep couch filled with over-stuffed pillows. The coffee table was topped with a hand-quilted table runner and a leather-bound copy of the Creator's Book of Instructions. In the corner of the room, under the quilt, sat a soft recliner. The comfortable décor helped Willow feel at home and at ease.

Knowing she was unable to stand for any length of time, the Creator encouraged Willow to sit in the recliner. As she sank down into the soft and soothing chair, she felt much of the pressure that had been weighing her down release. The Creator then kindly gave her what she needed most—time to rest. Willow slept soundly for many hours. When she awoke, she felt more at peace than she had in some time.

The Creator then introduced her to a close friend of His. This friend was a caring and intelligent doctor. She understood and believed that we are all "fearfully and wonderfully made" by our Creator's intricate design. Willow's new doctor was a great teacher as well. Willow learned how to prepare fresh food (provided by the Creator) and was given helpful medications. She was also encouraged to take small steps toward getting her body to move again. Willow considered her time with this doctor to be a great blessing. She listened intently and followed the physician's words of wisdom because she truly wanted to regain her health.

In every way, Willow benefited from her time in the Resting Room. She enjoyed the peace and stillness. She was especially fond of her uplifting conversations with the Creator. She loved to sit quietly by the fire reading from His Book of Instructions. The familiar words renewed her faith on a much deeper level.

As the pain from her illness began to subside, Willow was able to walk more easily. The Creator carefully observed her progress. When she was ready, the time had come for Him to deliver the first of many lessons she would learn in this home.

8
REST IN THE LORD

Early one morning, Willow headed toward the kitchen to prepare breakfast. As she walked through the Resting Room, she noticed that her Book of Instructions was left open on the coffee table. Luke 10:38–42 had been highlighted with a bright yellow marker. It was hard to miss. After making her breakfast, she returned to the couch and sat down. She picked up her Book and read the newly highlighted verses…

"As Jesus and his disciples were on their way, he came to a village where a woman named Martha opened her home to him. She had a sister called Mary, who sat at the Lord's feet listening to what he said. But Martha was distracted by all the preparations that had to be made. She came to him and asked, 'Lord, don't you care that my sister has left me to do the work by myself? Tell her to help me!'

'Martha, Martha,' the Lord answered, 'you are worried and upset about many things, but few things are needed—or indeed only one. Mary has chosen what is better, and it will not be taken away from her.'" (NIV)

Willow was quite familiar with this Bible lesson. She understood the importance of spending quiet time with the LORD even in the midst of a busy schedule. Willow thought about how she, like Martha, often allowed her attention to shift away from what mattered most.

She desired to do better and yet she didn't know where to begin. So, in the quietness of the Resting Room, Willow began to pray.

"Lord, show me the joy, peace, and comfort You want me to experience this day. Remove all distractions so that I may clearly see You and Your great plans for me."

She then read aloud from her Book of Instructions…

"Search me, God, and know my heart; test me and know my anxious thoughts. See if there is any offensive way in me, and lead me in the way everlasting." (Psalm 139:23–24 NIV)

Just as she finished her prayer, the Creator entered the room. He held a framed photograph in one hand and a hammer and nails in the other. He said nothing. He nailed the weathered wooden frame on the wall across from where she was sitting. As she looked at the photograph, it fascinated her. Bright reds, yellows, and oranges filled the sky as the sun lowered into the deep blue water of an expansive lake. In the center of the photo, an emerald green catamaran with clean white sails cut through choppy waves. Seagulls with wings wide open soared across the top of the picture. It was a tranquil scene that brought back memories of trips Willow had taken with her family many years earlier. She recalled the inner calm she experienced while sitting along a similar shore and how free she felt as she skimmed across the water on a catamaran very much like the one in the photo. Tears welled up in her eyes. (Thankfully, with her doctor's help and the Creator's healing, her tears had returned.) Willow missed those trips. She longed for serenity.

Willow daily felt the need to do more, be more, and plan more. She asked herself, "Why am I doing this? What is the point of racing through my life? It feels as though I can never do enough!" Knowing her thoughts, the

Creator invited her to join Him in front of the mirror that hung on the wall.

The mirrors that hung throughout this house were perfectly placed by the Creator. Each reflection would reveal a truth allowing Willow to see herself in His light. The Creator's mirrors were quite unlike the dark snake's deceptive Mirror of Comparison that spoke nothing but hurtful lies to Willow.

As they looked together into this first mirror, the Creator asked Willow what she saw. She truthfully responded, "I am looking at someone who has lost her focus. She enjoys pleasing people and has forgotten the importance of rest. I see someone who is now tired and sick."

He appreciated her honesty. He asked her to move once more, this time in front of the quilt hanging above the recliner. The design on the quilt was simple. Willow had looked at it numerous times while walking through the Resting Room and into the kitchen. It had a narrow border of buttercream yellow fabric and a background made up of light gray and purple squares. Her attention had always been drawn to the charcoal gray door that had been hand appliquéd near the center of the quilt.

With the Creator by her side, Willow paused to look at the quilt more carefully. For the first time she spotted tiny embroidered words hidden among the hand quilting on the dark gray door. They were almost invisible to the eye.

She read them aloud:

D isappoint

O thers,

O bligations,

R eputation, and

S trength to endure.

Willow noticed immediately that the first letter of each embroidered word spelled out "DOORS." This acronym was, of course, not an accident. It was another helpful tool lovingly given by the Creator to help Willow remember His valuable lesson. He wanted her to carry these insights far beyond the little brick house and all the way to her Great Eternal Reward.

The Creator began with an explanation. "The doors throughout this house will not only lead you to new rooms and lessons, but they are symbolic. They represent things that are holding you back from understanding your true identity as My beloved child. One by one, we will open these doors. As we do, lies will be destroyed and My truth will become clear."

Willow listened closely to His every word. Her heart was open and ready to receive.

He said, "I know that you long for serenity. You are tired and yet you still feel as though you need to do more. It is time for you to experience the joy that comes when you rest in Me."

He pointed to the quilt and said, "Let us take a few moments to talk about these words." He asked for her thoughts.

After pausing to consider, Willow responded, "Well, I guess I will begin with the first two words: 'Disappoint Others.' I do not like to disappoint people. In fact, I will do whatever I can to keep other people happy."

The Creator asked, "Even if it means setting aside your own needs?" She nodded.

He then asked, "And how well are you succeeding at keeping other people happy?"

"Not very well," Willow had to admit. "It is not only impossible, but exhausting!"

The Creator smiled, "That is because it is not your job to keep other people happy. Remember that I am Creator and Provider. I will supply the needs of all My children. While you may bring temporary happiness to others, their lasting joy is not based on anything you can do or furnish. True and unshakeable joy is a gift from My Spirit given to those who understand My great love and know the sacrifice My Son Jesus, made for them."

He went on, "It is good that you have a desire to bring happiness to others, but not at the cost of neglecting your own needs. It is My plan for you to not only care for others, but for yourself as well."

Willow took in and appreciated His words of wisdom. Rest and peace were available when she would learn to surrender her fear of disappointing others.

They went on to discuss the next word embroidered on the quilt: "Obligations." The Creator declared, "You have allowed yourself to become weighed down by numerous obligations. Many were never meant to be yours. Just as you were not created to keep every person happy, you also were not designed to be the solution to every problem.

I am pleased that you have a desire to serve those in need. There are times, however, when you have chosen to help, yet it was not *your* place or responsibility." She knew that He was right.

He continued, "You see, I have laid out opportunities for all of my children to experience the joy of serving. By following your own plan, you have unintentionally taken that joy away from others. Follow My lead. Help when you are called to help, but step back when others are called to share and use their gifts."

His words helped her to grasp another important piece of His beautiful and complex plan. If Willow would do the things the Creator had planned for her (no more and no less), there would be plenty of time for rest.

Willow then recalled reading about Mary and Martha. She said, "Many days I feel like Martha. I become easily distracted by all of the things that need to be done. I try to do too much and then end up losing my focus and joy of serving."

The Creator smiled. "You are not alone. Martha was upset and worried about many things. It was not wrong for Martha to want to make earthly preparations, but Mary chose what is better."

Willow quickly agreed. "Mary chose to set aside the obligations and the preparations so that she could do what was most important—spend time listening to Your Son, Jesus."

The Creator was pleased with Willow's response. He sensed her greater understanding of the truth. Their conversation continued as He moved on to the next embroidered word on the quilt: "Reputation."

He asked, "do you know the deeper reason why you do not want to disappoint others and why you feel the need to fulfill obligations?"

She could not answer and so He gently continued, "It is because you are concerned about your reputation. Please do not misunderstand. It is good and helpful to have an honorable reputation. Your reputation, however, should never become more important than My plans. You have spent too much energy striving to meet the demands of people rather than seeking My will and approval."

Willow could not help but agree. She felt sorrow for her misguided thoughts. The Creator's Spirit quickly offered forgiveness and peace. Willow once again recognized that she needed the Creator's help in every area of her life. She would never experience true rest until she learned to give up on her own efforts.

The Creator continued by explaining the last words embroidered on the quilt: "Strength to endure." He said, "Willow, I am here to help you—always. You are never alone. I have led you through many difficult obstacles on your journey. As you think about the new challenges that lie ahead, I want you to know for certain that I will give you strength to endure. You never have to rely on your own strength. I will give you what you need. Lean on Me and rest in Me."

The Creator concluded, "The photograph I hung on the wall earlier was meant to remind you that I have given you a beautiful place to live. If you allow Me to lead the way, your path will take you to many peaceful shores. Take time to stop striving and just be. Slow down. Look for the good gifts I have given you. Take a long walk, sit by the water, observe colors, breathe in the fresh air, and allow music to fill your soul. Treasure these moments and reflect on My love for you.

His words penetrated deep into her heart. She began to comprehend how important it was for her mind, body, and soul to rest in the LORD. She came to understand that it was only in the quiet moments, when she was removed from daily distractions, that she would be able to hear His still small voice and the beautiful messages He had prepared for her.

One afternoon, Willow leisurely sat and read from one of the books the Creator had selected for her. Her attention shifted as she watched Him stand and walk to the back of the room. He lightly pressed on the large bookshelf next to the fireplace. She was surprised to see it easily slide several feet to the right. As the bookshelf moved, a hidden door was revealed. The Creator said, "Willow, it is time for you to pass through the next door." Her heart excitedly skipped a beat at the thought of exploring beyond the Resting Room. The Creator knew the time had come.

9

STRENGTH AND WELLNESS STUDIO

"You are my strength; I wait for you to rescue me, for you, O God, are my fortress. In his unfailing love, my God will stand with me." (Psalm 59:9–10 NLT)

The Creator led Willow through the door and into the new room. As she stepped inside, she noticed a measurable difference. The Resting Room was warm and comfortable. This studio was brightly lit and had a more industrial feel. Willow recognized one of her favorite Christian bands playing in the background through the speakers located on either side of the room. The Creator knew that music inspired her.

This fitness center was equipped with floor to ceiling mirrors (something Willow had never learned to appreciate), shelves containing hand weights of all shapes and sizes, exercise balls, pulleys, and resistance bands. It also contained a treadmill, stationary bike, and floor mat. Her favorite part about the studio was the large picture window looking out onto the edge of the sequoia grove. Having a view of the Creator's handiwork helped Willow to relax in the midst of this more intense setting.

The Creator then introduced Willow to a new team of His helpers. They were known as Strength Builders. This group had been granted abundant wisdom in knowing exactly how to restore strength and motion to the physically weak. With the Creator leading the way, the Strength Builders would help Willow develop a plan to move more easily once she returned to the solid path.

Although she had already experienced much healing, Willow was concerned about her remaining limitations. She worried about her ability to push through a new exercise regimen. She prayed about her anxious thoughts.

The Creator requested for her to join Him in front of the wall of mirrors. He asked, "Willow, what do you see in these mirrors?"

She simply answered, "I see someone who is still weak. I'm sorry, but I don't think I can do this."

The Creator quickly reassured her, "Are you standing alone?" She shook her head.

He asked if she remembered the words embroidered on the quilt in the Resting Room and she acknowledged that she did.

He continued, "You *will* have the strength to endure. This strength will not come from inside of you. It will be My gift to you. There is no pressure here—no worry about disappointing others. The helpers I have given you are here to encourage, not judge. Release your expectations to Me. Rest in Me. Remember that when you are weak—I am strong. Lean on My strength to see you through."

He knew that worry still held her heart captive and so He said, "Let's go back to the Resting Room and read from My Book of Instructions." She felt great relief at His words and the thought of returning to the familiar room.

10

LEAN ON MY STRENGTH

They walked back through the door and into the Resting Room. He invited her to sit on the couch. After some quiet time, they read together the following account from Matthew 14:22–33:

"Immediately Jesus made the disciples get into the boat and go on ahead of him to the other side, while he dismissed the crowd. After he had dismissed them, he went up on a mountainside by himself to pray. Later that night, he was there alone, and the boat was already a considerable distance from land, buffeted by the waves because the wind was against it. Shortly before dawn Jesus went out to them, walking on the lake. When the disciples saw him walking on the lake, they were terrified. 'It's a ghost,' they said, and cried out in fear. But Jesus immediately said to them: 'Take courage! It is I. Don't be afraid.' 'Lord, if it's you,' Peter replied, 'tell me to come to you on the water.' 'Come,' he said.

Then Peter got down out of the boat, walked on the water and came toward Jesus. But when he saw the wind, he was afraid and, beginning to sink, cried out, 'Lord, save me!' Immediately Jesus reached out his hand and caught him. 'You of little faith,' he said, 'why did you doubt?'

And when they climbed into the boat, the wind died down. Then those who were in the boat worshiped him, saying, 'Truly you are the Son of God.'" (NIV)

When they finished reading the Creator said, "My Son, Jesus, who has power over all creation, miraculously enabled Peter to walk on the water in the midst of a storm. Why then, do you suppose, Peter began to sink?"

Willow answered, "It was his fear. When Peter took his eyes off of Jesus and noticed the wind and the waves, he became afraid and began to sink."

The Creator approved her answer and went on, "Willow, you are living through a storm now. I know that it is difficult to see beyond the wind and waves. I know that it is easy to let fear take over. But you have Jesus, the Rock, the One who walked on water and calmed the storm, on your side. Keep your eyes fixed on Him.

Isaiah the prophet wrote, "But those who hope in the LORD will renew their strength. They will soar on wings like eagles; they will run and not grow weary, they will walk and not be faint."[2]

"Do you know what it means to hope?" the Creator asked.

Willow had just recently led a youth study on this topic and so she confidently answered, "Hope is the expectation of great things to come."

"Yes." He agreed. "It is pleasing and right for you to place your hope in Me, not in yourself or in other people. Lean on Me for help through this storm. When you seek

---

[2] Isaiah 40:31 (NIV)

Me as your source of strength, you will run the race I have set before you and not grow weary. You have My power, My Son's saving grace, and My Spirit's wisdom all freely offered to you as you walk this journey toward the Great Eternal Reward."

His words were like the sweetest medicine to Willow's soul. She needed the reminder that, with her Creator at her side, she could expect great things to come.

He went on, "I am able to help and heal. Hold tight to the words written about Me in Psalm 147:3–5: 'He heals the brokenhearted and binds up their wounds. He determines the number of the stars and calls them each by name. Great is our Lord and mighty in power; his understanding has no limit.'" (NIV)

Willow did hold on tight to the Creator and His promises. Truthfully, she was too weak to make it on her own. She knew that she needed Him. As an added source of encouragement, He left His Book of Instructions open with a newly highlighted verse each day. Here are a few of the treasured Scriptures He shared with her:

"With man this is impossible, but with God all things are possible." (Matthew 19:26 NIV)

"The faithful love of the Lord never ends! His mercies never cease. Great is his faithfulness; his mercies begin afresh each morning." (Lamentations 3:22–23 NLT)

"Whoever dwells in the shelter of the Most High will rest in the shadow of the Almighty. I will say of the LORD, 'He is my refuge and my fortress, my God, in whom I trust.'" (Psalm 91:1–2 NIV)

Willow carefully followed the plans laid out for her. She grew to enjoy sessions in the gym, yet she also looked forward to quiet breaks back in the Resting Room. These were uplifting times, not just for Willow's body, but for her mind and soul as well. She came to understand the importance of depending on the LORD for strength. When she had fully grasped this truth, the Creator knew that she was ready for her next lesson.

11

MEADOW VIEW

One morning, as Willow exercised, the Creator called for her to join him near the back of the gym. He guided her through what she thought was a closet door. Willow was stunned by what she saw on the other side. The newly discovered room was only about fourteen feet deep, but it ran across the whole back length of the little brick house. Surrounded by windows on three of its four walls, Meadow View, as it was called, was bright and airy.

Willow hoped to spend a lot of time in this beautiful place. Without asking, she made herself at home on the richly woven brown wicker couch. She sank deep down into the plush sandalwood cushions. The Creator took joy in watching His child benefit from the plentiful gifts He had provided for her in this home.

The view of the expansive meadow through the opened windows was breathtaking. A quiet breeze produced a slight sway in the white lace curtains. As Willow shifted her focus back inside the room she noticed clean, stylish furniture. In addition to the couch where she was resting, there were two brown wicker chairs purposefully arranged for optimal viewing of the meadow. A small oval mirror was the lone adornment on the walls.

The colorful mural of the meadow painted along the back wall was almost as impressive as the actual view out the windows. Camouflaged within the mural were three doors. Willow felt certain that each of these doors would lead to another room and another lesson. Her heart filled with anticipation.

A coffee table rested in front of the couch. The table was topped with a stunning blue and green hand-blown glass vase filled with freshly picked flowers. Once the vase caught Willow's attention, she could not take her eyes off of it. She had never seen anything quite as remarkable.

In the back corner of the long and narrow room sat a well-used wooden workbench. While it did not match the stylish furniture, it settled into the room décor as though it had been custom built for that exact spot. Behind the workbench stood two cabinets filled with what looked like antique carving and woodworking tools. Having grown up around her dad's tools, Willow was familiar with many of the items she saw on the shelves.

Willow cherished her time in this room. She thoroughly enjoyed watching the birds and other little creatures playing outside. It delighted her to observe the Creator as He generously provided food for them.

One beautiful afternoon, Willow left the Resting Room to enjoy time in Meadow View. As she walked passed the table, she noticed that the Creator had highlighted another verse in His Book of Instructions. She looked forward to learning His next lesson.

She was just about to begin reading when the Creator took a seat at the old workbench. He reached for a chisel off the shelf and began whittling away on a large block of aspen. Willow was fascinated as she watched Him carve. She could only imagine what magnificent work of art He might be creating. She was unaware that the precious gift His hands were fashioning would soon become hers.

Willow shifted her focus back to the highlighted verse. She read, "For all the animals of the forest are mine, and I own the cattle on a thousand hills. I know every bird on the mountains, and all the animals of the field are mine."[3]

Before she even looked up from the page, He began, "It is all Mine, Willow. Every flower, every star, every animal, and every person—they belong to Me. I care for and understand every living thing I have made. I weave complex details together in perfect harmony. Concepts that are too difficult for the human mind to comprehend are plain to Me because I am the designer and architect of all creation. It is My great joy to provide for you.

David wrote, 'The eyes of all look to you in hope; you give them their food as they need it. When you open your hand, you satisfy the hunger and thirst of every living thing. The Lord is righteous in everything he does; he is filled with kindness. The Lord is close to all who call on him, yes, to all who call on him in truth.'"[4]

Without saying another word, the Creator walked over to the small mirror and encouraged Willow to join Him. He once again asked her what she saw.

Her answers were gaining in depth as she continued to learn from her time with the Creator in the little brick house. She answered, "I see someone who is loved and cared for by her awesome Creator. I see a person who is getting stronger and is learning valuable lessons. This

[3] Psalm 50:10–11 (NLT)

[4] Psalm 145:15–18 (NLT)

person continually needs improvements, but is heading in the right direction."

He was touched by her thoughtful answer. He then invited Willow to read these verses from Matthew 10:29–31:

"Are not two sparrows sold for a penny? Yet not one of them will fall to the ground outside your Father's care. And even the very hairs of your head are all numbered. So don't be afraid; you are worth more than many sparrows." (NIV)

Willow looked out at the meadow and saw several sparrows eating on the ground underneath the bird feeders. The Creator spoke, "Not a sparrow falls to the ground without My knowledge."

Willow wondered how that could be given the endless numbers of sparrows found in their meadow alone.

The Creator explained, "Willow, I am capable of knowing all things. I also know you. You are worth more than many sparrows. I may have made every part of this incredibly large universe, but I also know every minute detail about you. I know how many hairs you have on your head. I know your thoughts and your words before you even speak them. I know your heart and your future. Fully rely on Me. Allow Me to lead you through this journey. You, My daughter, are priceless to Me."

12

PRICELESS, NOT PERFECT

The Creator's words filled Willow's heart with admiration and excitement. She quickly closed her Book of Instructions and set it back down on the table.

Without looking, she inadvertently pushed the heavy book right into the beautiful vase. She watched helplessly as the treasured work of art wobbled and then toppled off the side of the table. As it hit the floor, hundreds of glass pieces bounced off the tile.

Willow loved that vase. Now it lay in many colorful pieces shattered all around the floor. She felt heartbroken. She could not stop the tears from flowing.

She cried out, "What a mess—just like me! Broken. Scattered. How could I be so clumsy?"

The Creator's Spirit did not allow Willow to sit long in her self-condemning thoughts before He provided these words: "Do not worry about this vase. It was an accident. Perfection is Mine alone. You are priceless, not perfect."

The Creator walked with Willow over to His workbench. He lifted the chisel covered in wood shavings and said, "I know that you have enjoyed watching Me work on this project." Willow nodded and then added, "I have. I cannot wait to find out what it will become. I know that when You are finished, it will be amazing!"

He smiled and continued, "I do have special plans for this ordinary block of wood, but it is still a work in progress. There are imperfections and unneeded portions that must be removed in order to form this piece according to My design."

Willow added, "That sure sounds a lot like me. I know that I am still a work in progress. I have imperfections and unneeded things in my life like busywork, guilt, and fear. These things need to be removed, or carefully chiseled away, because they are standing in the way of me fully becoming the person You designed me to be."

"That is a very wise conclusion," the Creator said. "You are progressing. There *are* things in your life that need to be released. I am in the process of chiseling away the unneeded. I must warn you that there will be times when chiseling hurts or seems confusing. Even then, I need you to trust that I know what is best."

The Creator then gently bent down and began to collect all of the broken pieces of glass on the floor. He placed them in an old wooden bucket and set them next to His workbench.

He shifted Willow's attention to the mural along the back wall of Meadow View. He said, "Willow, you were right to surmise that each of the three doors within this mural would lead to a new room. You have been prepared and are ready to receive the important lessons waiting for you. You are now free to come and go anywhere in this house."

13
HARMONY SUITE

Willow wasted no time setting foot in a new room. She chose the middle door of the three remaining. She was about to discover another remarkable gift, a place called "Harmony Suite." As she glanced around at the wide variety of musical instruments, she felt a wave of familiar contentment, a delight she had not felt in years.

You see, Willow had been born with a song in her heart. She sang, whistled, and played several instruments. She even tapped her fingers and toes when nothing else was available. Music lifted her spirits and enabled her to express her overflowing joy.

Sadly, somewhere along the way, the dark snake had stolen much of the pleasure Willow found in music. The Creator, in His limitless wisdom planned to use Harmony Suite to shatter the lies that held Willow captive. His truth would soon prevail.

Willow's wide eyes took in all that this well-equipped music studio had to offer. The suite was made up of three soundproof practice rooms. Each room had a large glass window, making it easy to view the vast inventory inside.

The first room held a black music stand, two chairs, a flute, and an old hymnal opened to "Just As I Am." The flute was not randomly chosen. It was Willow's very own student model, the one her parents bought for her in fifth grade. She knew it was hers because she could see the repair that had been made years ago when the silver finish had begun to wear off the mouthpiece. That little flute had been with Willow through grade school, high school, and college. She used it to play solos in worship services, weddings, and even at Christmas concerts in shopping malls. Many people encouraged Willow to continue playing—band directors, choir directors, family, and friends.

Regrettably, from the first time Willow played her flute in front of another person, fear entered her heart. She did not want to make mistakes. Despite all of the support and kind words, Willow focused on the squeaks, cracks, and missed notes (even when they were few and far between). She became her worst critic. The fear contaminated her joy and, eventually, she stopped playing. By the time she arrived at Harmony Suite, her flute had become dusty and disregarded.

A large mirror hung on the wall of this first practice room. Willow stepped up to take a look. The Creator quietly observed. He knew His Spirit would guide her. She could not deny that she saw the reflection of a musician. Music was a gift she had unquestionably been given. It was part of her identity—a part she had lost and sincerely wanted to regain. As Willow thought about her flute, she felt regret. She questioned why she would have allowed fear to take away something that was so important to her.

With a heavy heart, Willow moved on to the second room in Harmony Suite. This practice room featured top-notch recording equipment and an expensive vocal microphone. A picture hung on the wall just over the recording equipment. It was a picture of Willow as a little girl singing in the children's choir at their home church.

The Creator quietly walked up behind Willow. He asked what she thought of the picture. She did not want to answer. He knew the reason for her silence. He also understood why she, as an adult, still hesitated to sing in front of other adults.

The day of the children's choir concert, a teacher referred to her as "a little frog." Those words cut deep into a sensitive little girl's heart. Before that comment, she would sing freely from the bottom of her heart and at the top of her lungs. (Willow still experienced great joy in singing praises to the Creator, she just preferred for no one else to hear her.) Not only did Willow lose confidence in her singing voice the day of that concert, but she began to dislike her speaking voice as well.

The dark snake relished the opportunity to build on her lack of confidence. The Mirror of Comparison he placed in Willow's bag of details reminded her every day that she could not sing or speak as well as others. She grew ashamed of the way she sounded.

The Creator knew this would be a difficult yet important lie to shatter. The truth was He needed her voice in His Kingdom. It held great purpose and potential.

As they sat quietly in the second practice room, a recording of young Willow singing, "This Little Light of Mine" played through the speakers. Willow squirmed at the sound.

The Creator spoke, "Willow, your voice was masterfully created and lovingly gifted to you. It was designed to fulfill an extraordinary role in My Kingdom."

The song continued to play. "I want you to listen closely to the little girl on this recording. You may hear the missed notes. I hear the beauty of one of My precious children singing heartfelt praises to Me. The little girl on this recording was happy to let her light shine. That is, until someone stole her joy and told her she couldn't sing.

Many voices will speak lies to you, Willow. They will say things like, 'You are not good enough,' 'You should have done more,' 'You must perform without mistakes,' or 'You are not a writer.'

Only one Voice speaks truth. My voice tells you, 'You are loved,' 'You are a treasure,' 'You have talent,' and 'You are My masterpiece.' To which voice will you listen?" He asked.

She answered quickly, "I want to listen to You, but there are times when the other voices are so much louder than Yours."

He answered, "That is why it is so important for You and I to spend quiet time together each day. It is only in the quiet moments that you will be able to hear My still, small voice.

Many of My children expect to hear from Me in obvious ways—through earthquakes, wind, and fire. There may be times when I will speak to you in these ways. But there will also be times when you need to listen carefully for My whisper. There are many loud voices competing for your attention. They will often try to distract you from My truth. When you feel confused or uncertain, ask My Spirit for discernment and He will lead you."

Willow believed the Creator's words and sensed her own courage growing. Harmony Suite had taught her a powerful lesson and yet, before she could move on, there was one more significant truth to be shared. The Creator led her to the third practice room.

14

HIDE IT UNDER A BUSHEL? NO!

The third practice room in Harmony Suite was filled with many of Willow's old instruments. The one that stood out most was the guitar her dad bought for her while she was in college. There were also hand bells, a drum set, keyboard, mountain dulcimer (a gift from her sister), recorder, music stands, and other percussion instruments. All of these had been enjoyed by Willow somewhere along her journey.

The Creator stepped into the room with His Book of Instructions in hand. He shared, "I took great pleasure in listening to the music you created on each one of these instruments. It wasn't only your earthly father who was sad when you chose to stop using your gift of music. Willow, what was the name of the children's song we heard in the last practice room?"

She answered, "This Little Light of Mine."

"Right," He said, and then prompted her to look at the music stand where He had opened His Book of Instructions. He asked her to read Matthew 5:14–16.

"You are the light of the world. A town built on a hill cannot be hidden. Neither do people light a lamp and put it under a bowl. Instead they put it on its stand, and it gives light to everyone in the house. In the same way, let your light shine before others, that they may see your good deeds and glorify your Father in heaven. (NIV)

He then asked, "What do these verses mean to you?"

Willow replied, "We have faith in You and are loved by You. You have gifted each of us with talents. These gifts should not be hidden. Instead, we should let our light shine. We should share our faith, our talents, and Your love with the world."

The Creator went on, "You couldn't have said it any better. Now, I want you to live the words you have spoken. Do not hide your gifts. Use your voice for Me. Rediscover your joy of music."

15

SWEET HARMONY

As they sat together in the third practice room, the Creator went on to ask Willow, "Do you know what the word 'harmony' means?"

Willow made an attempt to answer. "It is when someone sings a part slightly different than someone else and it sounds really good together."

The Creator smiled at her understanding. He added a little more. "The melody carries the song. The harmony moves along at the same time together with the melody. The two parts form chords that are pleasing to the ear."

He explained further, "On your journey, I desire to take the lead. I will carry the melody. When you play the part I have written for you, your life will become a beautiful harmony, pleasing to Me. I will give you what you need. Together we will create sweet harmony."

Willow cherished the thought of letting her Creator take the lead, the melody. She wanted to follow His lead and produce a beautiful harmony by following the song He had written for her life.

She felt an overwhelming desire to do what she had not done in years—release the song in her heart once again—without fear or reservation. She looked around at all of the instruments in the room. She could not wait to play them all, but she went to the drums first. Even as a little girl, she could never pass up an opportunity to play the drums.

It did not take long before she was playing loud and strong. She gave it all she had. It felt like such a healthy way to release energy. Right down to her very core, she knew that she was doing exactly what she was born to do. She played fearlessly. She played so boldly, in fact, that she could not even hear the crashes of thunder, heavy winds, and pouring rain occurring right outside of the little brick house.

Willow was sheltered in the arms of her loving and almighty Creator who had returned to her the precious gift of music. The Creator was proud of her progress and looked forward to helping this dear child to grow even stronger in the days ahead. The time had come for Willow to open the next door and move on to a new room and a new lesson.

16

THE POTTER'S WHEEL

Although it felt longer, Willow had spent less than one day in Harmony Suite. She treasured her time there. She would now enjoy music as much as she had learned to enjoy resting in the Lord, exercising, and observing the animals out in the meadow.

Willow left Harmony Suite and returned to Meadow View. She looked at the large mural along the back wall and knew that she still had two more rooms to discover. The next door she selected was the one furthest away from the Strength and Wellness Studio. As she entered, her first impression of this room was that it was very small. One window and one lamp provided light to the entire place. As she looked out the window, she noted that it was foggy and drizzly outside (following the strong storms she never heard). The gray weather helped to explain the somewhat gray and damp atmosphere inside this room.

Looking around Willow spotted a potter's wheel, clay, a sink with buckets, towel, string, and other assorted tools she could not name. Willow knew nothing about throwing pottery. Actually, any form of art felt like a lost cause to her.

Hanging up on the walls, Willow noticed a mirror and a picture she had drawn as a child. She could not help but shudder when she saw her artwork on display. It wasn't just the picture—she felt uncomfortable in this room. She was contemplating whether or not to leave when the Creator entered and asked her to join Him by the picture.

As she looked at her childhood project He said, "I am well aware that this room makes you uncomfortable."

"Yes. It does. I am not an artist, as You know." She replied pointing at the example of her early art hanging on the wall.

"I have heard you share that with many people through the years," He responded. He then lightly placed His hands on her shoulders and turned her so that she could only focus her eyes on His rather than on what she perceived as a failed attempt at drawing.

As quickly as worry tried to enter Willow's mind, the Creator's Spirit replaced it with peace. Looking into His eyes, Willow was reminded that in her weakness, He is strong. She set aside her presumptions and quietly listened.

The Creator proceeded to give Willow an assignment, "I would like you to create something special for the meadow. It can be whatever you would like. As you create, keep in mind the lessons we have learned. I have placed instruction books and pottery guides on the bookshelves back in the Resting Room. Feel free to research as desired, but please, Willow, do not seek perfection. Take your time. There is no pressure. Create from your heart. I will bless your efforts."

This was the first art project that Willow looked forward to completing. She decided that her first task would be to identify something needed in the meadow. This gave her a good excuse to return to her favorite room in the house. Even through the light rain and fog, Willow loved watching the animals busily gathering food. She noticed a taller tree stump standing about three feet off of the ground. She looked around for birdbaths and saw only one. She decided to create a second bath for the birds of the meadow and planned to place it on top of the tall stump.

The next step was to look for design ideas. Willow left Meadow View and went to the Resting Room. As promised, the Creator had supplied every book necessary to teach her how to create a ceramic birdbath. She looked in gardening magazines for ideas. She researched necessary tools and learned the steps to be taken when working with clay.

She spent many days researching, watching the birds in the meadow, and designing at the potter's wheel. She developed a relaxing rhythm to her work. As promised, the Creator blessed her efforts. She followed His instructions. She created from her heart and was not concerned about flaws.

She took her time diligently working the clay. She formed a large flat platter with a shallow lip around the edges. She purposely placed a bump in the center of the bowl because she thought that the tiny birds might like to stand in the middle of the water. Once it was finished, she gently set it on a shelf to dry. At just the right time, when the clay was leather hard, the Creator took care of firing Willow's piece of art for the first time. She then selected a deep green glaze to match the green meadow. When she was pleased with the way it looked, the Creator took her project back to the kiln. He finished it for her and returned it to the potter's wheel. She felt pride and a sense of accomplishment. With His help, she had done something she never thought possible. She had to admit that the little birdbath was everything she hoped it would be. She couldn't wait to watch the birds of the meadow enjoying it.

The Creator joined Willow in admiring her work of art. He then asked some unexpected questions. "Willow, what if I told you that this birdbath did not want to be green? What if it did not even want to be a birdbath? Suppose I told you that this birdbath admired all of the pitchers in the kitchen and would have rather been a pitcher. How would you feel?"

At that moment, Willow wanted to laugh but she saw that the Creator was quite serious. She focused back in on His questions and sincerely pondered what seemed ridiculous.

After much thought she answered, "But I was the designer. The birdbath was simply my work of art. The birdbath has no right to tell me how I should have made it or suggest what it would have rather been. Willow smiled because she was very quickly beginning to understand the Creator's point even as she spoke.

The Creator also smiled because He knew she was grasping another one of His significant truths. He gently turned the birdbath upside down to reveal words He had inscribed: I am the Potter and you are the clay.

He then asked, "Have you always been happy with who you are?"

She answered honestly, "No. Not at all."

He continued, "You are My masterpiece. I am pleased with who I made you to be. My work in you is not finished. I continue to mold you as you walk on your journey. You are designed exactly as I want you. You fit flawlessly into the assignment I have for you. No one could possibly do it better than you."

He looked again at her handiwork and said, "This birdbath was created from your heart and it is beautiful. It serves its purpose.

You were created by Me and you are beautiful. You are here to fulfill your purpose. You do not need to be the best artist or singer if it is My desire for you to write. Similarly, if My purpose for you is to teach, then you do not need to be the best construction worker, waitress, or accountant. All purposes are equally important. You only have to be what I have made you to be. Listen to Paul's inspired words from 1 Corinthians 12:17–20:

'If the whole body were an eye, where would the sense of hearing be? If the whole body were an ear, where would the sense of smell be? But in fact God has placed the parts in the body, every one of them, just as he wanted them to be. If they were all one part, where would the body be? As it is, there are many parts, but one body.' (NIV)

You are one part of many. I have arranged all parts just as I want them to be. All are needed. All are significant."

The Creator then asked Willow to step over to the mirror on the wall. He asked her yet again, "What do you see?"

This time, the Creator's Spirit gave Willow the wisdom to take in all of the truths she had been taught. At that very moment she was given a clear picture of her true identity. And so, with a strong and full voice, Willow proclaimed the truth, "I see wonderful Willow, a precious child of the One True King."

The Creator put His arm around her and said, "Yes, Willow. You are wonderful and you are loved." He rejoiced at her words. These were the words He had longed to hear her speak.

Willow would soon be ready to explore the last room in the little brick house. But before she could enter that room, the Creator had still more planned for her.

17

GARDEN BENCH

Willow was invited to walk with the Creator through the meadow. She had not been outside since the first day she entered the house. She could hardly wait to breathe in the fresh air, smell the wildflowers, and watch the birds enjoying the birdbath she had designed for them.

As He carefully carried her masterpiece, the Creator allowed Willow to lead the way. He felt her joy. When they arrived at just the right spot, she pointed to the chosen tree stump and He firmly set the birdbath in place. She turned to take a few steps back in order to get a better look at her completed work of art. As she turned, she spotted a garden bench resting between the tall grasses. She stared at the beautifully carved wooden bench. When she looked more closely, she saw colorful glass pieces forming the words "Wonderful Willow" inlayed into the top of the bench.

Tears welled up in her eyes as she thought back to the days spent in Meadow View. She loved to watch the Creator carve away on what appeared to be an ordinary piece of aspen. That ordinary piece of wood had now become this garden bench—an extraordinary gift made especially for her. She couldn't help but ask herself, "Who am I that the Lord of heaven and earth would make such a gift for me?" At that very moment she felt treasured. The only words she could speak through her tears were, "Thank you. This is exceptional."

The Creator asked her if she recognized the glass pieces. As He spoke, she remembered breaking the beautiful vase that rested on the coffee table in Meadow View. The Creator had cleaned up the broken pieces, collected them in an old bucket, and set them aside. She had no idea what He planned to do with them. To her they were nothing more than useless fragments. He, however, had greater plans. Willow was made aware, once again, that He makes all things beautiful in His time—even her.

The Creator spoke, "Willow, I work all things together for good. When you see broken, I see beautiful. When you see flawed, I see potential. Even your illness, in My hands, has become a gift. What the dark snake meant to cause harm, I have used as a tool to help you. Your illness has forced you to be still (to cease striving). In the quiet times, you have learned to depend on Me for answers. You have been reminded, once again, that in your weakness, I am strong.

During our time in this home, I have taught you many valuable truths. We have opened many doors together and, in so doing, we have shattered many of the dark snake's deceptive lies.

My dear child, it is almost time for us to return to the solid path. Do not be afraid to leave this place of refuge for I will continue to walk with you on your journey. You will never be alone. You are treasured." He encouraged her to hold on to these verses:

"I took you from the ends of the earth, from its farthest corners I called you. I said, 'You are my servant'; I have chosen you and have not rejected you. So do not fear, for I am with you; do not be dismayed, for I am your God. I will strengthen you and help you; I will uphold you with my righteous right hand." (Isaiah 41:9-10 NIV)

18

WILLOW'S SONG OF THANKSGIVING

Willow did not feel concern when she thought about leaving the little brick house. Instead, she felt an overwhelming desire to give praise to her Creator for His great love, His awesome gifts, and the cherished lessons she would carry with her for the rest of her days.

She asked Him to wait on the garden bench while she went back into the house. He willingly consented, already knowing what she had in mind.

Willow walked into the home and went back into Harmony Suite. She picked up (and dusted off) her flute. She also picked up the Book of Instructions still resting on the music stand. She carefully pushed together the three silver pieces of the familiar old instrument and headed back out to the meadow. The Creator beamed with pride as He watched her walking back toward Him.

She began by singing the following verses from David's Psalm:

"Let all that I am praise the LORD; with my whole heart, I will praise his holy name. Let all that I am praise the LORD; may I never forget the good things he does for me." (Psalm 103:1–2 NLT)

The melody effortlessly flowed from deep within her soul as if the song had been written and rehearsed for years. She felt no shame in sharing her voice with Him. On that day, she was not at all concerned about missing notes. There was nothing but joy.

Willow then went on to play her flute. Her hands easily remembered the fingerings. The sounds of her worship soared over the gentle sounds of the meadow. Willow gave all that she had praising her Creator. He gladly accepted her gift of love.

19
FOUNDATION

Willow knew that her days in the little brick house were coming to an end. She continued to spend precious time each morning sitting on her bench in the meadow watching the birds. She valued those moments to reflect on all that she had learned during her time of rest.

One sunny afternoon, the Creator asked Willow to walk with Him out in the meadow. She gladly agreed. She loved their walks and talks.

After a long stroll and pleasing conversation, they headed back in the direction of the house. Willow noticed, however, that the Creator took a slightly different route this time. She willingly followed. They had not gone far before coming upon another house. Looking at the impressive building, Willow could not help but feel she had seen it before. After struggling to remember, she finally recognized it as the extravagant home she was first offered as a place of refuge. As you may remember, Willow did not select this larger home because it had been foolishly built on a foundation of sand.

Willow looked closely at the big house and noticed a deep crack near its shifting foundation. The whole house looked as if it might crash into a heaping pile of rubble at any moment. The storms that had blown through weeks earlier were more than the home's foundation could handle. Willow's little brick house, built on the Rock, easily and safely handled those very same storms. Willow, in fact, had never even heard the storms as she boldly played her drums in Harmony Suite.

The Creator spoke to Willow, "My dear child, you learned much from your battle against the great big rock. You have learned even more during our time in the little brick house. I brought you here to show you what happens when My children rely on anything other than Me. People and things are My gifts to you but they cannot hold you up. Only I have the strength to help you safely weather any storm.

Listen to what the psalmist says:

'God is our refuge and strength, an ever-present help in trouble.' (Psalm 46:1 NIV)

Willow, I will not keep you *from* trouble. I will be your ever-present help *in* trouble. You *will* face more storms in your life. There will be things that attempt to shake your very foundation. But when you build your life on Me, your Rock, I will keep you safe and secure."

Finally, He said, "Before we return to the solid path, I must caution you that the dark snake is not finished lying to you. He will continue to slither past and feed you lies. He will often try to distract you from Me. Sometimes you will not even be able to recognize his cunning tricks. But hold onto this good news—I fight your battles. When you feel down, weak, worthless, or broken, turn to Me for truth. Keep your eyes fixed on Me. I am stronger than anything the dark snake can set in your path. Hold on to My words:

'What shall we say about such wonderful things as these? If God is for us, who can ever be against us?'" (Romans 8:31 NLT)

20

WRITER'S DESK

Willow continued walking with the Creator until they returned to the little brick house. Together they went to Meadow View and stood in front of the large mural. The Creator said to her, "The time has come for you to discover the last room in this house. Please step inside."

Willow opened the final door. The room was unadorned. It contained a heavy wooden desk, a lamp, a journal, a pen, and a small mirror. A note sitting on the desk read, "This is NOT YOURS." Willow wondered at the meaning of these words.

It had been quite a journey. Willow had entered the little brick house feeling quite ill and believing the dark snake's lie that told her she was not a writer.

One room at a time, the Creator had patiently walked with her on a strength-building journey. He offered love, guidance, and help every step of the way. She had been granted restored health, renewed faith, and a greater understanding of her identity.

Despite all of the progress that had been made, in His infinite wisdom, the Creator knew that one more task remained. Willow could not yet fulfill His great plans for her until one more lie was defeated.

Willow felt safe in the new, small room. She sat at the desk and picked up the notebook. She loved nothing more than a fresh journal. It held a world of possibilities. It was an empty slate. Truth be told, she LOVED painting pictures with words. It was a cherished gift from her Creator.

As she sat at the desk, she caught the reflection of herself in the small mirror. The Creator did not stop to ask her what she saw. This time, He told her. This is what He said: "You are wonderful Willow. You are Mine. You have a unique and important testimony that needs to be shared. Write about what you have learned."

He then turned away from the mirror and looked directly into her eyes. "You do not need to worry about pleasing others with your stories. You do not write alone."

He continued, "It is not up to you to make people believe or accept the words you write. Allow My words to accomplish what I desire and achieve the purpose for which I send them. This is NOT YOURS.

As it says in Isaiah 55:11: '…so is my word that goes out from my mouth: It will not return to me empty, but will accomplish what I desire and achieve the purpose for which I sent it.'"(NIV)

Willow felt honored to place words on a page that represented the beautiful images and lessons her Creator had shared with her.

And so, for the first time in months, Willow once again believed that she *was* indeed a writer. With that realization, another one of the dark snake's lies was shattered.

Following the Creator's lead, Willow filled page after page with His truths. Under His direction, Willow wrote the book you now hold in your hands.

21
RETURNING TO THE SOLID PATH

It was time for Willow to leave the little brick house where she had learned so much. It was difficult for her to even recall how greatly she was suffering the first day she entered the home in the arms of her Creator. She had forever been changed by the quiet time spent with the LORD.

This place of refuge had been a great gift to her. Not only had she gained renewed strength and restored health, but she now also carried a new confidence because she understood her true identity. She was wonderful Willow, a precious child of the One True and Living God.

The Creator carefully led Willow away from the house, back through the sequoia grove, and returned her to the solid path. She felt at peace following His lead. She kept her eyes fixed on Him.

Though she knew there would be storms ahead, Willow had once again been reminded that she would not need to face them alone. Her Almighty Creator would fight her battles. In moments of weakness, His strength would see her through.

The great big rock and the little brick house had taught Willow the importance of building her life on Jesus, her Rock and Strong Foundation.

CONCLUSION

So now, dear reader, it is time to ask you – What do you see when you look in a mirror?

Do you see someone who is…

    …not enough?

        …a mistake?

            …hopeless?

                …flawed?

*Always remember that the One who knows all things created you.

> "How precious to me are your thoughts,
> God! How vast is the sum of them! Were I
> to count them, they would outnumber the
> grains of sand." (Psalm 139:17–18 NIV)

*You were made with a purpose that is yours alone.

> "'For I know the plans I have for you,'
> declares the LORD, 'plans to prosper you
> and not to harm you, plans to give you hope
> and a future.'" (Jeremiah 29:11 NIV)

*You are loved and saved.

> "For God so loved the world that he gave
> his one and only Son, that whoever
> believes in him shall not perish but have
> eternal life." (John 3:16 NIV)

*You are God's work in progress.

> "He who began a good work in you will
> carry it on to completion until the day of
> Christ Jesus." (Philippians 1:6 NIV)

*You are His wonderful masterpiece!

"For we are God's masterpiece. He has created us anew
in Christ Jesus, so we can do the good things he planned
for us long ago." (Ephesians 2:10 NLT)

ABOUT THE AUTHOR:
TRUTH BEHIND THE STORY

While some of Willow's experiences and emotions belong to the fictional character alone, the basic story line follows the life of the author. Tammy Schwartz has served as a Director of Christian Education since 1998. She, like Willow, considers it a great privilege to share God's love and His Word with people of all ages. She cherishes time spent with her sister, two nieces, McKenna and Paige, dear family, and many good friends.

Tammy wrote her first short story, "The Great Big Rock" in 2017. Soon after that, she began to battle an unidentified illness. After months of tests and doctor visits, she was diagnosed with Sjogren's Syndrome and Rheumatoid Arthritis. The illnesses left her temporarily unable to work. During a three-month medical leave, Tammy spent much time talking with the Lord in the quietness of her own "little brick house." Though difficult, those days were not wasted. Many of the lessons she learned are contained in the pages of this book.

These days, Tammy is thankful for progress made, strength restored, truths revealed, and lies defeated. With the help of the LORD, she has been led to believe that she is a treasured child of God (And so are you)!

> "Now all glory to God, who is able, through
> his mighty power at work within us, to
> accomplish infinitely more than we might
> ask or think." (Ephesians 3:20 NLT)

STUDY QUESTIONS & JOURNAL
(for small group or personal use)

<u>INTRODUCTION</u>

1. Name five things you love most about God's creation.

2. What does God's handiwork tell you about who He is and how He feels about you?

3. On a scale of 1 to 10, how do you feel about the person God created you to be?

1	5	10
I am a mess		I am a masterpiece

<u>Journaling</u>: (Choose one.)

-Write down three things you like about yourself or three things you do well. Thank God for the person He made you to be.

-Write a note asking God to help you find the beauty and value in who you are.

CHAPTER ONE – Willow's New Path

1. When do you most feel as though you are walking a level path with God at your side? (Examples: in worship, at home with family, fishing, etc.)

2. Which statement best describes you? Explain.

    a. I can do this on my own.

    b. I will let you know when I need help, Lord.

    c. I fully trust You. I can't do this on my own.

3. In what ways would you benefit from surrendering every detail of your life over to the LORD? What stops you?

<u>Journaling</u>:

-Make a list of things that are currently filling up your time and stealing your peace. Talk to God about your list and ask for help in surrendering all of your burdens over to Him.

<u>CHAPTER TWO</u> – A New Purpose

1. What are we privileged to do according to 1 Corinthians 1:3–5? Discuss a time in your life when you were able to follow these verses.

"Praise be to the God and Father of our Lord Jesus Christ, the Father of compassion and the God of all comfort, who comforts us in all our troubles, so that we can comfort those in any trouble with the comfort we ourselves receive from God. For just as we share abundantly in the sufferings of Christ, so also our comfort abounds through Christ." 1 Corinthians 1:3–5 (NIV)

2. Willow felt led by the Lord to begin writing her life story. Has God been placing new and exciting ideas or plans in your mind? Do you feel as though He has been encouraging you to step out into a new area of ministry, a new relationship, a new job, etc.? Explain.

3. What holds you back from carrying out God's "new" plans for you?

<u>Journaling</u>:

-Write a list of actions (or ideas) that God has recently placed in your mind. Pray over them and ask God to help you to know which of these actions are His plans and what next steps you need to take.

<u>CHAPTER THREE</u> – An Old Enemy

1. Do you carry your own Mirror of Comparison? When are you most likely to compare yourself to others?

2. The devil (dark snake) is a liar. He relishes the thought of getting you to doubt yourself. What lies have you believed lately? How can these lies be defeated?

3. Willow had a difficult time accepting forgiveness. Is it easy for you to accept forgiveness from God? From others? Why or why not?

<u>Journaling</u>:

-Make a list of people (do not share) you have forgiven or need to forgive. Also make a list of people who have forgiven you. Pray over these names, remembering Ephesians 4:32: "Be kind and compassionate to one another, forgiving each other just as in Christ, God forgave you." (NIV)

CHAPTER FOUR – A Deep Dark Valley

1. Which is most true for you:

    a. I focus on compliments and criticism equally.

    b. I tend to focus more on compliments.

    c. I tend to focus more on criticism.

2. Has criticism ever held you back from doing the things you know you were meant to do? Explain.

3. What do we learn from 1 Thessalonians 2:4?

"For we speak as messengers approved by God to be entrusted with the Good News. Our purpose is to please God, not people. He alone examines the motives of our hearts." (NLT)

<u>Journaling</u>:

-Write about a time when you sought the approval of other people but experienced rejection instead. How did you feel? Ask the Lord to heal the hurt of rejection and replace it with His truth. He loves you unconditionally, today and always!

CHAPTER FIVE – Place of Refuge

1. Have you ever doubted your purpose for being on this earth? What (or who) has helped you to remember that you are here for a reason?

2. Read Psalm 121. Write down words that are especially meaningful to you.

3. How does it help you to know that you are never alone in fighting your battles or facing struggles?

<u>Journaling</u>:

-Make a list of ways that God has already used you to build up His Kingdom. Say a prayer of thanks for these opportunities and ask the Holy Spirit to prepare your heart for what is yet to come.

<u>CHAPTER SIX</u> – I Will Carry You

1. Think about a time in your life when you really needed rest. Describe what was happening and how you felt.

2. The Creator gave Willow her choice of two homes as her place of refuge. Do you think most people would have chosen the large, impressive home or the little brick house? Why?

3.   Which home would you have chosen? Please explain.

<u>Journaling</u>:

-Write about and thank God for your favorite place of refuge.

<u>CHAPTER SEVEN</u> – The Resting Room

1. Do you tend to move to the Creator's time or your own? Why?

2. The Creator provided Willow with a kind and intelligent doctor at just the right time. What people has God placed in your life at the exact moment you needed them?

3. What prevents you from "sitting quietly, reading from the Bible?" Ask God to remove these obstacles from your life and fill you with the desire to seek His truths daily.

<u>Journaling:</u>

-Write about a time when God gave you what you needed more than anything else. Take a moment to thank Him for His love and provision.

<u>CHAPTER EIGHT</u> – Rest in the Lord

1. Do you tend to be more like Mary (knowing the importance of spending quiet time with the Lord) or Martha (being distracted by the many things that need to be accomplished)? What steps can you take to be more like Mary?

2. Which of the following are true in your own life? How would each statement impact your ability to experience God's peace?

> a. I do not want to disappoint others. I like to try to keep people happy.

> b. I am sometimes overwhelmed by obligations.

> c. There are times when my own reputation has been of more importance to me than God's plans (In other words—I have cared more about what people think of me than what God has planned for me.)

3. Share a time when you felt certain that God had given you the strength to endure.

<u>Journaling</u>:

-Look through your calendar for the coming weeks and intentionally write in times to rest in the Lord. You may want to begin your quiet times with this simple prayer:

Lord, show me the joy, peace, and comfort you want me to experience this day. Remove all distractions so that I may clearly see You and Your great plans for me. In Jesus' name I pray. Amen.

<u>CHAPTER NINE</u> – Strength and Wellness Studio

1. Think about your own daily interactions. When or where do you feel the most vulnerable (weak)?

2. In moments of weakness or vulnerability, how does it help to know that you do not stand on your own?

3. Who are the "Strength Builders" in your life? (People who know just what you need to keep pushing forward.) Take a moment to thank God for them.

<u>Journaling</u>:

-Meditate on the following Bible verses and write down your thoughts:

> "You are my strength; I wait for you to rescue me, for you, O God, are my fortress. In his unfailing love, my God will stand with me." (Psalm 59:9–10 NLT)

<u>CHAPTER TEN</u> – Lean on My Strength

1. Peter walked on the water toward Jesus until he noticed the wind and the waves. When fear took over, he began to sink. How often does fear stop you from doing the great things God has planned for you? What steps can you take to fight against fear?

2. Hope is the expectation of great things to come. As a child of God, what are you hoping for?

3.What strength do you draw from Psalm 147:3–5?

"He heals the brokenhearted and binds up their wounds. He determines the number of the stars and calls them each by name. Great is our Lord and mighty in power; his understanding has no limit." (NIV)

<u>Journaling</u>:

-Make a list of fears you are facing right now. Pray and ask the LORD for the strength to defeat these fears. Remember—you are not standing alone.

CHAPTER ELEVEN – Meadow View

1.   Willow immediately made herself comfortable in Meadow View. The Creator took joy in watching her benefit from the plentiful gifts He had provided for her. How often do you take time to recognize the plentiful gifts God has provided in your life?

2.   How does it make you feel to know that God knows every minute detail about you?

3.   What do these Bible verses mean to you?

"For all the animals of the forest are mine, and I own the cattle on a thousand hills. I know every bird on the mountains, and all the animals of the field are mine." (Psalm 50:10–11 NLT)

<u>Journaling</u>:

-Spend quiet time sitting outside or looking out a window. Observe and take notes describing God's amazing creation.

 – Priceless, Not Perfect

1. Do you tend to be hard on yourself when you make mistakes? Why or why not?

2. True or False: "You are priceless, not perfect." Explain. How might these words provide comfort?

3.   Have you sensed God chiseling anything out of your life? How do you feel about that?

<u>Journaling</u>:

-Write about a recent accident or mistake. Express your shame, guilt, and/or sorrow to the Lord. Ask Him to replace your negative thoughts with His unshakeable peace.

<u>CHAPTER THIRTEEN</u> – Harmony Suite

1. How easy or difficult is it for you to hear God's Voice
(the truth) over the voices in this world? Explain.

2. The hymnal in Harmony Suite was opened to the old
hymn, "Just as I Am." How does it help you to know
that God loves you just as you are?

3. True or False: God needs your voice in His Kingdom.
Explain.

<u>Journaling</u>:

-Make a list of loud voices that do not always speak truth in your life. Ask the Lord to quiet these voices and to give you ears that are willing and able to hear Him.

<u>CHAPTER FOURTEEN</u> – Hide it under a bushel? No!

1. How do you feel about sharing your God-given talents with others?

2. Are you hiding any talents at this time? Explain why or why not.

3. Make a list of ways that you can let your light shine.

<u>Journaling</u>:

-Write down your thoughts as you read Matthew 5:14–16:

"You are the light of the world. A town built on a hill cannot be hidden. Neither do people light a lamp and put it under a bowl. Instead they put it on its stand, and it gives light to everyone in the house. In the same way, let your light shine before others, that they may see your good deeds and glorify your Father in heaven." (NIV)

CHAPTER FIFTEEN – Sweet Harmony

Thinking of your life as a song…

1.   How comfortable are you allowing God to write your song? Is He the melody or do you continually try to take the lead?

2.   Are you (the harmony) moving along at the same time as God (the Melody)? Do you ever "get ahead" of God's plans? Explain.

3.   What words would you use to describe the song God has written for your life? (Be creative.)

<u>Journaling</u>:

-Write out a plan (be as specific as possible) describing when, where, and how you will release the song in your heart once again. Describe how you will let go of fear in order to rediscover a lost joy. Ask the Lord for His guidance and His plan before you begin writing.

<u>CHAPTER SIXTEEN</u> – The Potter's Wheel

1. Willow had no skill, interest, or knowledge working with clay. Think about and share a seemingly impossible task that you were asked to complete.

2. How have you made it through difficult tasks in the past? What tools (things, people, thoughts, etc.) did God provide to assist you in completing these challenges?

3. Have you always been happy with the person you are? How does it help to remember that you are God's masterpiece, uniquely designed for His purpose?

<u>Journaling</u>:

-Describe a masterpiece you have designed. Write about the process, the time you spent creating, and your feelings about the finished work. Thank God for the care He took in creating you.

CHAPTER SEVENTEEN – Garden Bench

1. Willow was surprised by the beautiful gift of a garden bench. God grants amazing blessings to us every day of our lives. Share a recent gift that was especially meaningful to you. (Examples might include healing, success at work or school, relationships restored, a thoughtful handmade item, etc.)

2.   God works all things together for the good of those who love Him. What difficult things has God used for good in your life? (Example: Making it through an illness and then being given the opportunity to help someone facing a similar challenge.)

3. What important truths do we learn from Isaiah 41:9–10?

"I took you from the ends of the earth, from its farthest corners I called you. I said, 'You are my servant'; I have chosen you and have not rejected you. So do not fear, for I am with you; do not be dismayed, for I am your God. I will strengthen you and help you; I will uphold you with my righteous right hand." (NIV)

<u>Journaling:</u>

-Write a prayer asking God to help you see beauty beyond your brokenness.

<u>CHAPTER EIGHTEEN</u> – Willow's Song of
Thanksgiving

1. In what ways can you show thanks and gratitude to
the Lord?

2. In Willow's "Song of Thanksgiving" she sang, "May I
never forget the good things he does for me." (Psalm
103:2 NLT)

-How often do you remember to thank God for His good
gifts?

<u>Journaling</u>:

-Write a long and detailed list of God's gifts to you. Take time to thank Him for His love and provision.

<u>CHAPTER NINETEEN</u> - Foundation

1. What things have threatened to shake your very foundation?

2. What does it mean to build your foundation on the Rock?

3. What are the clear benefits of leaning on the Lord rather than leaning on people?

<u>Journaling</u>:

-When we look at our culture today, we see many people relying on everything but God. Write about the signs you have seen of foundations cracking. Pray for those who have not yet turned to Jesus.

CHAPTERS TWENTY AND TWENTY-ONE –
Writer's Desk & Returning to the Solid Path

1. The Creator left a note for Willow on the Writer's Desk which read, "This is NOT YOURS." It was a reminder to her that God was in control—He would lead her in writing her story. Where might God place a "This is NOT YOURS" note in your life? Are there any areas where you need to be reminded that He is in control?

2. Willow was also reminded that she would continue to face trials and temptations. What tools did Willow have to help her? What tools do you have to face future trials and temptations?

3. Willow was not afraid to leave the little brick house and return to the solid path. Why? How would you have felt when leaving?

<u>Journaling</u>:

God says to you: "You are wonderful ___________ (your name here). You are Mine. You have a unique and important testimony that needs to be shared."

-Write down truths that the Lord has taught you through Willow's story.